Look and Find®

STAR WARS
THE LAST JEDI

W9-AUI-556

pi kids® **Phoenix International Publications, Inc.**
Chicago · London · New York · Hamburg · Mexico City · Paris · Sydney

we make books come alive™

Rey isn't giving up hope. Luke Skywalker has refused his lightsaber — and the responsibility that goes with it. But the galaxy needs someone to bring balance to the Force. So Rey stays on Ahch-To and learns about life on Luke's island.

As the Caretakers prepare a meal, find Luke, their guests, and the things they never leave home without:

R2-D2

Rey

Luke's compass

Chewie's bowcaster

Luke

Rey's quarterstaff

Chewie

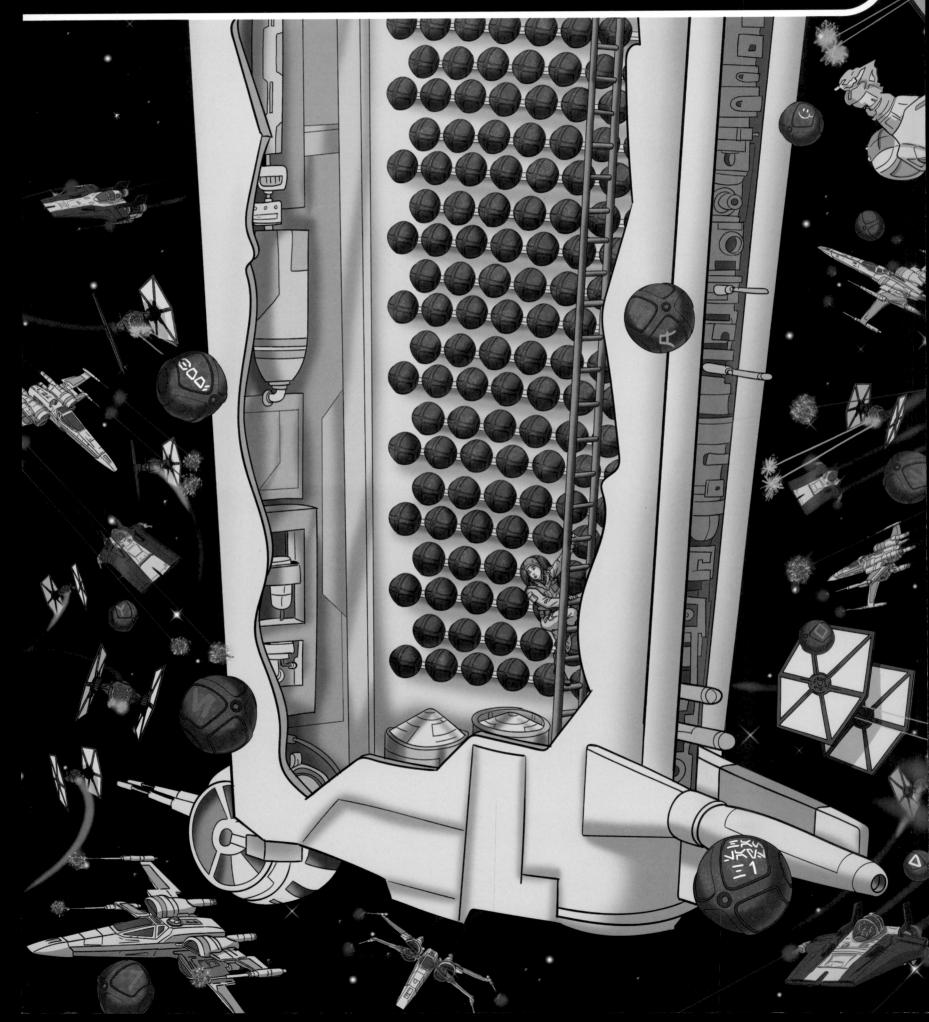

The Resistance needs to lose the First Order, FAST! Paige and her squad of heavy bombers lead the attack against the massive Dreadnought *Fulminatrix*. Paige's bomber may be small in comparison, but the damage she intends to do won't be.

Before Paige sends her *explosive* regards to the First Order, find these bombs:

Turn to the back of the book to translate these messages.

General Leia Organa discovers that the First Order's new technology can track her ship through hyperspace. But she and the Resistance maintain that spark of hope that keeps their cause alive. Kylo Ren and General Hux intend to snuff out that spark.

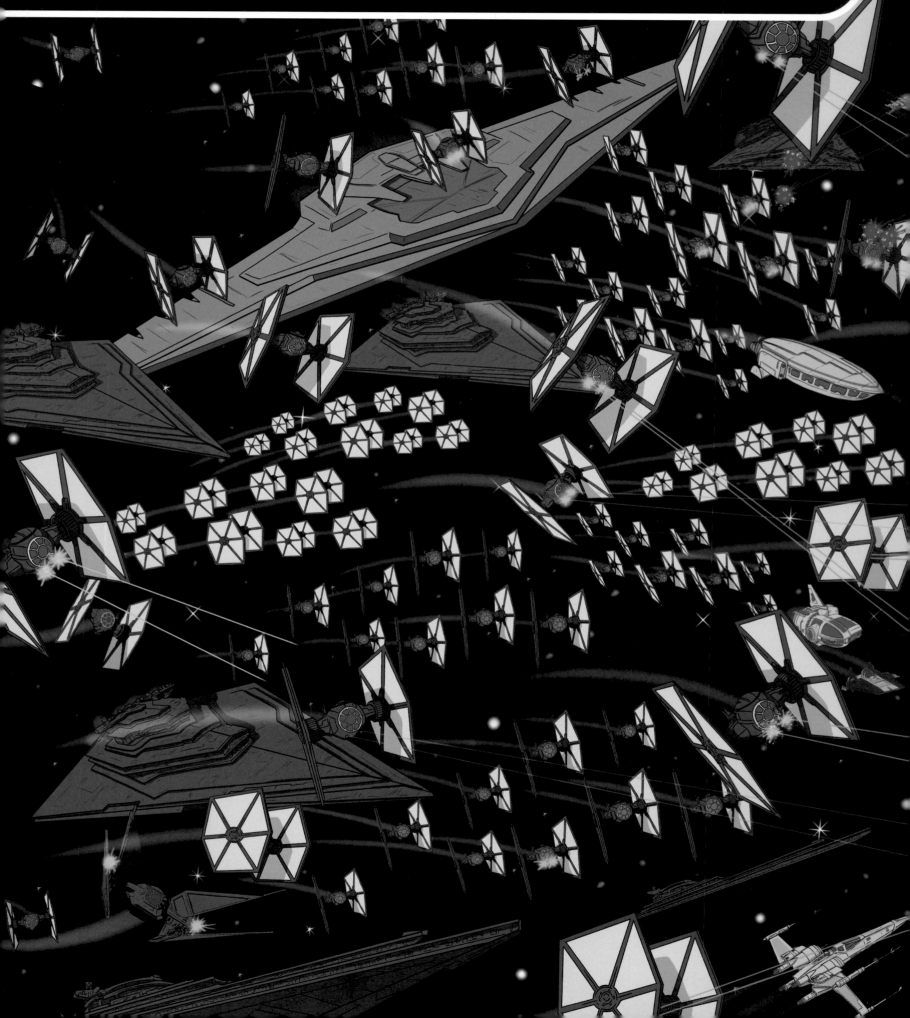

Help the Resistance keep ahead of these First Order ships:

Mega-Destroyer   this TIE fighter   TIE silencer   this TIE fighter   this Star Destroyer   this TIE fighter   this Star Destroyer

Every time Chewie lets his guard down, the porgs flutter all over him. Onboard the *Millennium Falcon*, Ahch-To's mischievous avian creatures have gotten themselves into plenty of trouble...and circuitry!

Help Chewie round up these porgs before their feathers clog the alluvial dampers:

Rey has waited patiently outside Luke's hut. She wants him to teach her the ways of the Force, but the old Jedi is reluctant to get involved again. Once Luke does open up, Rey quickly learns to feel the Force.

Reach out and find these things that belong to the Jedi Master:

bowl

ponipin astrogator

spear

roe-salve jug

salvaged
X-wing S-foil

S-foil clutch
actuator disc

mirrored
grooming box

fishing spear

The Canto Bight casino is a glitzy, glamorous game room filled with some of the galaxy's wealthiest—and a Master Codebreaker. Finn and Rose try not to stick out, but it doesn't take a Canto Cop to spot them...

Look for the man with the red plom bloom on his lapel and these other casino patrons:

Rose and Finn need to escape! Good thing the fathiers' stable boy is sympathetic to the Resistance. He releases the powerful, majestic animals, helping Finn and Rose make a quick—and destructive—getaway through the streets of Canto Bight.

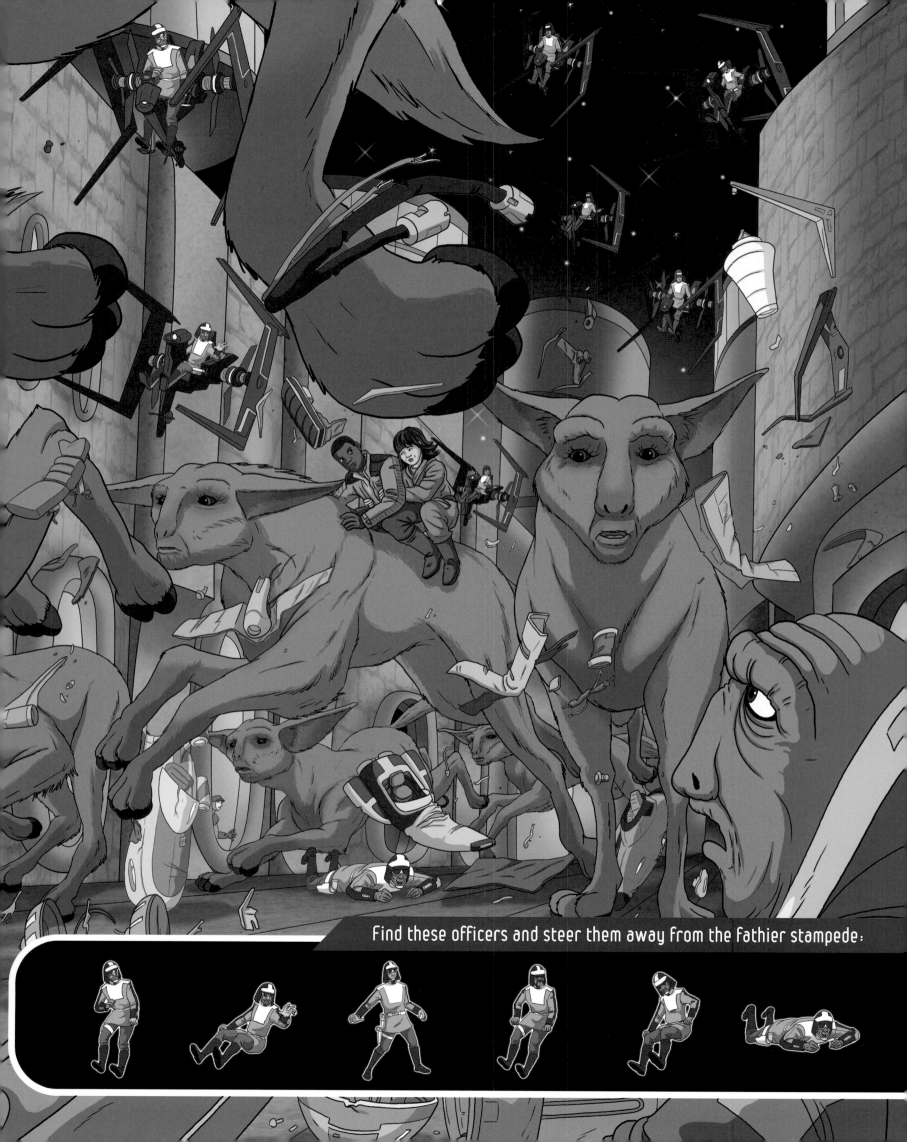

Find these officers and steer them away from the fathier stampede:

Red crystals erupt through the ground of planet Crait as the Resistance faces off against the First Order. They are outnumbered, have outdated technology, and are running out of time before their base's blast doors give out. But that doesn't mean they're giving up!

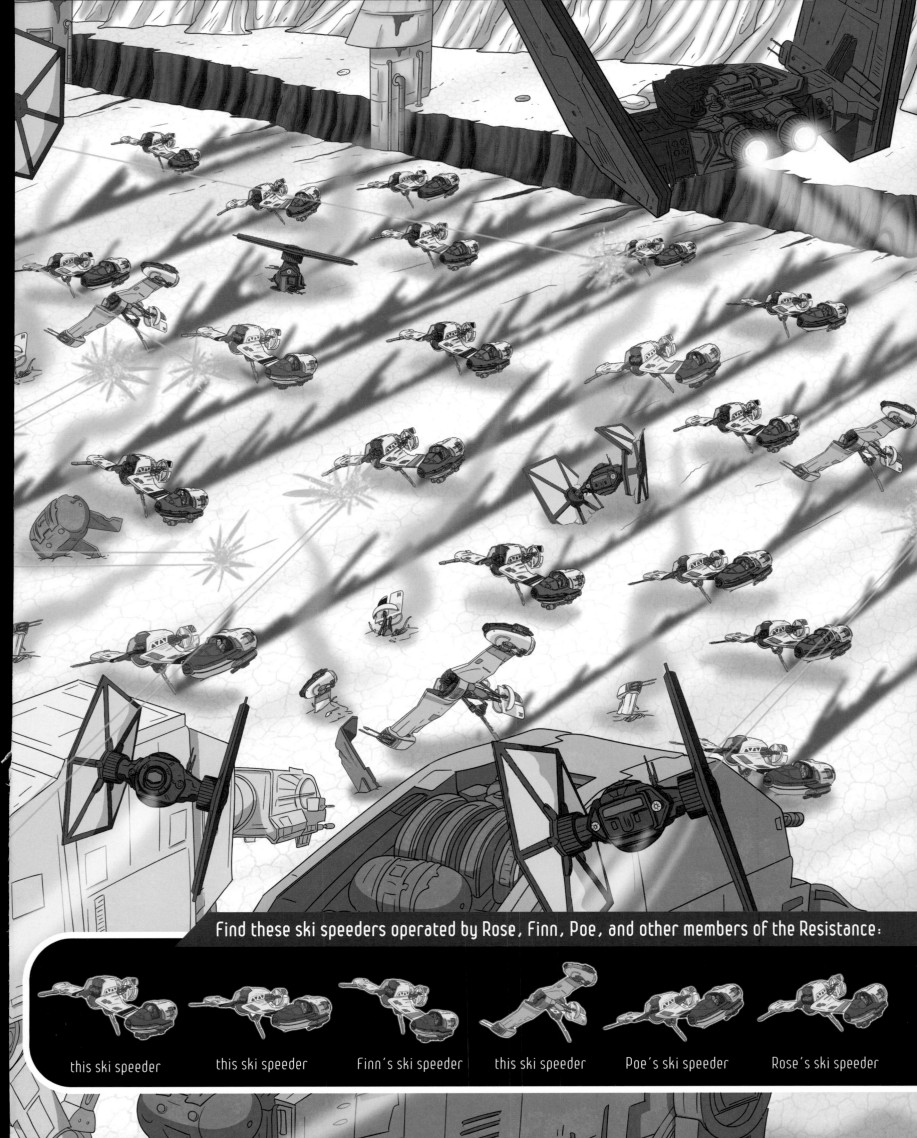

Find these ski speeders operated by Rose, Finn, Poe, and other members of the Resistance:

this ski speeder　　this ski speeder　　Finn's ski speeder　　this ski speeder　　Poe's ski speeder　　Rose's ski speeder

Travel back to Ahch-To and meet these Caretakers who maintain the ancient Jedi site:

Defeat the First Order! Blast back to Paige's bomber and find the Aurebesh letters that spell RESISTANCE:

Aurebesh Key

ᘉ	ᔔ	ᑕ	ᄀ	ᑊ	ᄓ	ᖯ	ᗐ	1	ᐢ	ᗌ	ᄂ	ᘔ
A	B	C	D	E	F	G	H	I	J	K	L	M

ᑫ	ᗠ	ᒪ	ᒪ	ᄀ	ᄓ	ᖚ	ᖁ	ᗌ	ᗊ	△	ᐃ	ᐱ
N	O	P	Q	R	S	T	U	V	W	X	Y	Z

Jump to the battle in space and find these Resistance ships:

the *Anoydyne*

this A-wing

this Resistance shuttle

this X-wing

Poe's X-wing

Resistance transport pod

the *Raddus*

The *Millennium Falcon* isn't just a bucket of bolts—it's also a hunk of junk stuffed with memories. Hit the hyperdrive and find these relics from past adventures. Punch it!

Mantellian Savrip · breath mask · helmet with blast shield · training remote · Han's welding goggles · "borrowed" stormtrooper comlink · comlink headset · bonding tape

Luke's diet on Ahch-To consists mainly of fish. Having lived in the Jakku desert nearly all her life, Rey is interested in the island's aquatic creatures. Help her find some tasty ones back at Luke's hut:

Roll the dice back at the casino, and see how many tokens you can find:

Ride back to Canto Bight and survey the wreckage in the fathiers' wake:

  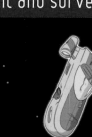 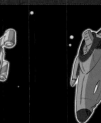  

The Resistance never misses a chance to chip away at the First Order. Cruise back to Crait and spot these bits of damage to the TIE fighters and walkers: